Wilderness Walkers

Naturalists in Early Texas

Wilderness Walkers

Naturalists in Early Texas

Written and Illustrated
by
Betsy Warren

Aline Speer
Research Assistant

Hendrick-Long Publishing Company

Dallas

Warren, Betsy.
  Wilderness walkers.

  Bibliography: p.
  Summary: Brief biographies of twelve naturalists
who studied the plants and animals of early
nineteenth-century Texas. Includes a glossary of
terms.
    1. Naturalists—Texas—Biography—Juvenile
literature. [1. Naturalists. 2. Texas—Biography]
I. Title.
QH26.W37   1987   574′.092′2 [B] [920]   87-12082
ISBN 0-937460-26-5

920
War

Copyright © 1987 Hendrick-Long Publishing Company
P.O. Box 25123
Dallas, TX 75225

Contents

Preface

Today's frontier is outer space. Scientists accompany exploratory space flights in order to collect samples of what they find. These specimens are then returned to earth, studied, and identified in scientific laboratories.

The frontier of the past was the land. Following the discovery of America, naturalists came here with the same curiosity and courage as our pioneers of space have had in going to the moon.

The naturalists who came to Texas were looking for new forms of plant and animal life, for mineral deposits, and for fossils that might furnish clues to the nature of life thousands of years ago.

An early naturalist often suffered severe hardships in his search. He had to make his way through a wilderness where there were no bridges over rivers, where a road was little more than a footpath. Hostile Indians were an ever-present danger, and illness often developed from insect bites, scarcity of food, or harsh weather conditions. Floods and storms carried away valuable tools and important collections. But perhaps the hardest part to bear was the loneliness. Illiterate settlers were highly suspicious of a stranger who spent his time digging up plants, catching insects, and packing frogs in alcohol.

What was it that caused these wilderness walkers to endure? Surely they did not expect great fame or money or immortality. It is more likely that these men were intrigued by the "unknown," and that they liked nothing better than observing nature close at hand to find out its secrets.

The stories of these seven scientists have intrigued us, the authors, for more than four years. Their contributions to our knowledge of Texas increase in value when one walks those hundreds of miles with them through the wilderness.

Betsy Warren
Aline Speer

Jean Louis Berlandier
1805(?)–1851

DAY PRIMROSE
Calylophus berlandieri

Jean Louis never did know the date of his birthday. No one had thought to write it down. He was born on a farm near Geneva, Switzerland, to parents who were too poor to send him to school for long. However, lack of schooling could not stop Jean Louis from learning. He made up his mind to teach himself about the things he wanted to know by reading books.

In Geneva young Jean Louis ran errands for a pharmacy. He soon learned how to collect and dry plants for the doctors and pharmacists, who made them into medicines. Before long Jean Louis had learned to use the scientific Latin names for each medication and could write them on labels that were pasted on the medicine bottles.

In spare moments Jean Louis taught himself to read Latin and Greek from borrowed books. When he was not reading or collecting plants, he was making friends with people who came into the pharmacy. One of the customers was a well-known teacher of botany at the Geneva Academy—Professor DeCandolle. It seemed to the professor that a boy who could teach himself to read two new languages would also be a good scholar. DeCandolle asked Jean Louis if he would like to attend botany classes at the academy to learn more about plants.

Jean Louis soon became one of the best students in the school. He excelled not only in his studies but also in drawing flowers and animals with utmost accuracy.

Before long the academy professors asked him to go to the city of Marseilles, France, on a special errand. They wanted him to pick up a live ostrich that was being sent from Africa to the museum in Geneva. Off went Jean Louis. He met the ship at Marseilles, put the ostrich in a crate, and carried it in a wagon back to Geneva without mishap. The professors were pleased. The young Jean Louis just hoped that he would have more such adventures.

And very soon he did. When Jean Louis was

RED BRUSH
Lippia berlandieri

about twenty years old, the academy professors asked him to go to the new Republic of Mexico to find out about the plants and animals there. They offered to pay him to collect samples, make drawings, and send everything back to them in Switzerland. After classifying and naming these specimens for their museum collections, they would then write articles and books about them. They were eager to be the first scientists to tell the world about the latest discoveries in Mexico. Also, they would sell any extra samples to other academies, botanical gardens, and private collectors.

With his usual enthusiasm, Jean Louis packed his bags. Exploring a new country and maybe meeting some Indians too were exactly the kind of adventures he liked.

ACACIA
Acacia berlandieri

In December 1826 Jean Louis sailed from France across the Atlantic Ocean, landing near Tampico, Mexico. As soon as he got off the ship, he began gathering mollusks and shells along the shore. He put dozens of them in barrels and sent them back to the academy in Geneva. During the next few months, he explored the countryside all the way to Mexico City. Because no one he met could understand the French, Latin, or Greek that he spoke, he learned Spanish, the language spoken in Mexico.

In Mexico City Jean Louis visited with a Mexican general named Mier y Terán. Their meeting had been arranged in a letter from Professor De-Candolle. Jean Louis had heard that Mier y Terán was about to lead a group of men on an expedition to the land held by Mexico north of the Rio

TEXAS TORTOISE
Gopherus berlandieri

Grande. DeCandolle hoped that his student would be able to go along with the general to make studies of the land.

"The land is called Coahuila y Texas," Mier y Terán said in his visit with Jean Louis. The general warned Jean Louis that there were unfriendly Indians roaming over the land looking for buffalo and plants to eat, and that strangers who traveled through the Indians' hunting grounds risked having their horses stolen.

It sounded like another fine adventure to Jean Louis. He was eager to go along so that he could hunt plants and animals for his collections and study the Indians. The general said that Jean Louis could join the expedition if he brought his own horse and provided his own food by hunting in the rivers and fields along the way. These conditions were agreeable to Jean Louis.

As for the general, he had a job to do for Mexico. Government officials had asked him to go up to the Sabine River to find out just where Mexico's land stopped and the land of the United States started. He had been given orders to determine a boundary line between the two countries. Also, he would be busy directing the expedition, which would include his secretary,

SOFT GREEN-EYES
Berlandiera pumila

5

two doctors, one mineralogist, two commissioners, one map maker, and forty soldiers. As there were few roads in Coahuila y Texas and maps were scarce, Mier y Terán would have to study the stars to determine the direction to get to the Sabine. Jean Louis knew how to do this, and he promised to help the general find the way. He bought a sturdy horse and packed his bags.

A partial list of what Jean Louis packed might have read as follows:

> *packets for seeds and plants*
> *tweezers*
> *sharp knife*
> *sheets of paper for drying plants*
> *magnifying glass*
> *digging tool*
> *drawing paper, pencils*
> *2 heavy boards for pressing specimens*
> *books on botany and natural history*

WOLFBERRY
Lycium berlandieri

A wagon driven by a soldier carried supplies and baggage for the travelers. General Mier y Terán rode alone in a large, ancient coach. The other men rode on horses or mules and wore wide-brimmed hats for protection from the sun.

In November 1827 the expedition left Mexico City. It took the men thirteen weeks to travel 739 miles to the town of Laredo on the Rio Grande. Although Laredo was a small, desolate-looking village, everyone was glad to rest there awhile. The horses were exhausted from pulling the general's heavy coach over bumpy trails and from getting stuck in the mud when it rained. The men were eager to wash their clothes and catch some catfish in the river.

In the fields around Laredo, Jean Louis made his first collection of Texas plants. He also made his first drawings of Texas Indians when a large band of Lipans rode into town. The Lipans wore buffalo robes and feathered headdresses, carried bows and lances, and had brightly painted faces. Jean Louis admired their colorful appearance and determined to learn more about Indians in Texas.

After two weeks in Laredo, the expedition started out again for San Antonio. They saw no

TURKEY HAWTHORNE
Crataegus berlandieri

CACTUS
Enchinocereus berlandieri

7

houses along the way—only coyotes, wolves, and large herds of deer, wild horses, and buffalo. The first night, the men camped in tents by La Paría Creek. They were very cold and tired, but sleep was impossible while bullfrogs croaked all night-long from the creek banks. Jean Louis had neither seen nor heard a bullfrog before. He caught several and preserved them in jars of alcohol to be sent back to Switzerland.

Deep in the wilderness, the men found an unusual "post office" by the side of the trail. It was a large buzzard that someone had shot and nailed to a tree. Under its wide-spread wings was a piece of parchment that held information and directions to distant settlements.

Continuing toward San Antonio, the expedition came to the Nueces River. The water was so high from recent rains that the horses had to swim across. The men made a raft and loaded it with their baggage. It took all day and many trips to carry the baggage across the river. That evening a large flock of wild turkeys roosted in trees near the water. Jean Louis shot two of them for supper. While the turkeys roasted over the campfire, Jean Louis helped General Mier y Terán calculate the position of the camp by looking at the stars that appeared through the evening haze.

FIDDLEWOOD
Citharexylum berlandieri

On February 25, 1828, the men and horses crossed the Rio Frio. Near the river were hills and woods filled with wildflowers, butterflies, live oaks, and walnut trees. Carrying his sharp knife and magnifying glass, Jean Louis left the camp to gather samples. He arranged many plants between sheets of paper and cardboard in order to preserve their shape as they dried. Later he would wrap them between heavy boards to press them flat. He also filled dozens of packets with various kinds of seeds. These were the beginnings of a large collection to be sent back to the botanists in Switzerland.

When the expedition reached San Antonio a few days later, Jean Louis saw four old Spanish missions where priests had tried to teach Indians how to be farmers and Christians. The missions were now deserted and tumbling down, but they were still beautiful. Jean Louis wrote about them

MEXICAN BADGER
Taxidea berlandieri

9

in his journal. He also collected great numbers of butterflies and plant specimens near the missions.

As the expedition headed northeast toward the Sabine River on April 14, the wheels of the baggage wagon broke near the town of Columbus. Everyone was frustrated and annoyed. Jean Louis stopped grumbling long enough to go out into the countryside to look for more seeds, plants, and birds while the soldiers repaired the wheels.

After fixing the wagon, the men proceeded to San Felipe, a small town on the banks of the Brazos River. Torrents of rain had caused the Brazos to rise above its banks so that the wagon and coach could not cross it. The travelers had to wait two weeks for the water to go down. During this time Jean Louis looked up a famous person— Stephen F. Austin, who had brought the first families from the United States to settle in Texas.

SPANISH GRAPE
Vitis berlandieri

Even though he lived in a two-room log cabin with dirt floors, Mr. Austin had a fine library with 47 volumes of an encyclopedia. While Jean Louis was in San Felipe, if he was not gathering wild plants, then he was probably sitting on Mr. Austin's front porch reading about natural history from the encyclopedia.

The expedition left San Felipe on May 9. Unhappily they camped two days later at the Jared Groce plantation, near present-day Hempstead. It had rained so much that the wagons and coach had stuck in the mud, and mildew spoiled the food supply. Even more disastrous for Jean Louis, his plants rotted from the dampness, and water rising by the camp carried away most of his papers and specimens.

ASH TREE
Fraxinus berlandieriana

Mr. Groce gave food to the hungry men while his workers repaired the supply wagon. But the expedition had two other problems that he could not solve: the hordes of mosquitoes that bit everyone at night, and the gadflies that stung them during the day. Even the general was red-faced, swollen, and miserable from the bites.

Ordinarily Jean Louis would have been eager to catch mosquitoes and gadflies for his collection. But now he was no longer in the mood. In fact he became so ill with malaria that General Mier y

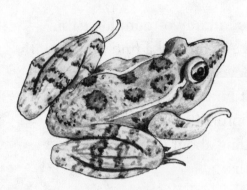

**RIO GRANDE
LEOPARD FROG**
Rana berlandieri

Terán made a bed for him in the coach and had several soldiers take Jean Louis back to San Antonio to a doctor.

Several weeks later Jean Louis was well and ready to begin collecting again. As it was too late for him to join General Mier y Terán at the Sabine, he gathered supplies and started for Aransas Bay from San Antonio. Indians stole his horse and belongings as he slept in camp the first night. He had to walk for two hours back to San Antonio to buy a new horse and more supplies. After all these troubles, one might think Jean Louis was ready to give up collecting. But two days later he was on his way to Aransas Bay, gathering plant and animal specimens as he went. These were shipped back to Professor DeCandolle in Geneva.

Jean Louis continued to have adventures all his life. One time he explored around the San Saba

River for lost silver mines. Another time he went with eighty Comanches to hunt for bear and buffalo near the Pedernales River. While living with the Indians for an entire month, he drew pictures and wrote long articles. These were later made into a book—*Indians in Texas in the 1840s.*

Jean Louis must have believed that he could have more adventures in Texas and Mexico than in Switzerland. He decided to live in Matamoros, Mexico, and become a doctor. Like other doctors of those times, he mixed his own medicines from plants he gathered himself. Townspeople, and especially the poor, trusted Doctor Berlandier and went to him when they were ill.

Jean Louis married and raised a family at Matamoros. For his children and for his studies of wild animals, he kept a zoo with an ocelot, coyotes, and wolves in the back yard of his home.

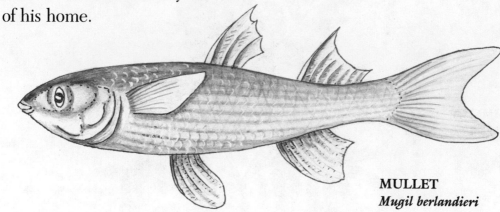

MULLET
Mugil berlandieri

When he was not busy studying, collecting, or practicing medicine, Jean Louis wrote. He wrote hundreds of pages about his botanical discoveries as well as the book about the Texas Indians. Some of his original writings and collections are in the Smithsonian Institution today and also in more than 25 other schools, institutions, and museums in America and Europe.

In 1836, while Texas and Mexico were at war, Jean Louis was put in charge of a hospital in Matamoros. He also acted as an interpreter for

MIMOSA
Mimosa berlandieri

Mexican generals who needed to talk to Texans. By now Jean Louis spoke English as well as Spanish, so he was a great help as an interpreter.

He had long ago stopped sending plants, animals, and mollusks to the Geneva Academy. Professor DeCandolle, sitting in his comfortable office in Geneva, complained that Jean Louis had wasted his time and the academy's money by sending only small collections, some of them in poor condition. DeCandolle could not begin to imagine how difficult it had been for Jean Louis to live and work in a wilderness where there were no roads, bridges, stores, or post offices. However, the list of specimens Jean Louis sent back to Geneva speaks for itself today: 198 packets of seeds, 935 insects, 72 birds, 55 jars of material in alcohol, 700 specimens of land and freshwater mollusks, and 188 packets of dried plants holding 55,077 specimens.

LAND SNAIL
Praticolella berlandieriana

In later years scientists recognized Jean Louis as a pioneering collector in Texas by naming plants and animals after him. Because of his findings, other naturalists came to make discoveries of their own. But today Jean Louis Berlandier is remembered and honored as one of the earliest educated naturalists to come to Texas.

Areas where Berlandier made his collections.

15

Thomas Drummond
1790–1835

WILD ONION
Allium drummondii

It was no wonder that Thomas Drummond grew up to be a naturalist. As a young boy in Scotland he learned how to care for plants while working in the gardens of an estate near his home. And his older brother was director of the Botanical Gardens in Cork, Ireland. Thus it often happened that Thomas heard about green, growing things. What he especially liked to hear were stories about the kinds of plants being discovered in a new country—America.

In the United States the study of native plants and animals by scientists was just beginning. The people of the young country were busy building new homes and new lives. Life there was different than life in Scotland, an old country where

17

people had long been settled in towns and on farms. In Scotland Thomas was able to go to school, where sometimes he read about the great, wide continent of America. He wondered if he would ever get to see the plants that grew there.

As it turned out, Thomas's first chance to go to America came in 1825, when he was 35 years old. He was invited to be part of a five-man British expedition in Arctic America. His job was to gather samples of plants and birds in the mountain wilderness of western Canada. For two and a half years Thomas collected specimens, traveling

RAIN-LILY
Zephranthes drummondii

WESTERN SOAPBERRY
Sapindus drummondii

18

CACTUS
Opuntia drummondii

up and down rivers and
across lakes in a large canoe
with an Indian as his guide. Sometimes he drove dog sleds or walked
on snowshoes hundreds of miles over crusty
snow four or five feet deep.

Once, when his boat became stuck in the ice,
Thomas's food supply ran out. To keep from starving, he ate the bird skins he had carefully preserved to be sent back to Scotland as specimens.

Once a huge angry bear, thinking Thomas had
come too close to her little cubs, attacked him.
And once Thomas was so hungry that he ate a
skunk—after cooking it, of course. "It gave me a
comfortable meal," he said.

In spite of all these difficulties during a year
and a half in Canada, Thomas took many hundreds of plant, seed, and bird specimens as well
as 286 kinds of moss back to Britain. When he got
home, he wrote two long books about the mosses.

SKULL-CAP
Scutellaria drummondii

To this day his work *Musci Americanus* remains helpful to scientists who want to study the mosses of Canada.

People liked Thomas and respected his work. The city of Belfast, Ireland, asked him to be manager of its botanical gardens in 1828. Thomas might have been happy there for quite a while, but another chance came to go to America in 1829. The Botanical Society of Glasgow, Scotland, offered to pay Thomas to make collections of previously unknown plants and animals in the United States.

On this trip Thomas walked or rode on horseback all over the eastern and southern United States while he looked for plants. For three years he was paid for gathering specimens to send back to England and Scotland.

While looking for plants around St. Louis, Missouri, Thomas heard his American friends talk about Jean Louis Berlandier, the first naturalist to make large collections of plants and animals in Texas and Mexico. When his friends showed him a set of the plants discovered by Berlandier, Thomas made a decision. He determined to go to Texas to see things for himself.

In May 1833 Thomas sailed into the Texas port of Velasco. Only about twenty or thirty people

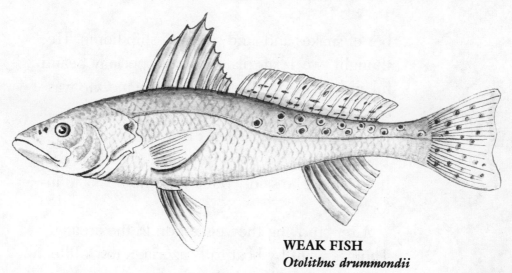

WEAK FISH
Otolithus drummondii

lived in the rough little village of four houses that
looked more like sheds. Rivers had flooded all of
the lowland around Velasco, making wide swamps
of waist-deep mud. Even so, Thomas managed
to find enough plants to make his first shipment
from Texas to scientists in Britain.

And then, like almost everyone else in Velasco,
he became ill with cholera in a plague that was
spreading around the world. Many people in
Velasco died from cholera. Others were too sick
to help Thomas get food or medicines. Although
close to starving, Thomas slowly recovered and
went out into the fields once again to collect
specimens. All in all, he gathered 100 species
of plants, the skins of 60 birds, and a great num-

OLD MAN'S BEARD
Clematis drummondii

ber of snakes and land shells to ship home. He thought two Texas plants were especially beautiful and wrote to a friend about them. One was coreopsis; the other, a copper-colored variety of the gaillardia, also called Firewheel or Indian Blanket. "I could ask a thousand questions about my plants," he said, "but I have no books to inform me."

After studying the vegetation in the area, Thomas went by boat to Brazoria, a town fifteen miles distant. The whole town was flooded from the waters of the Brazos River, and the floor of the boardinghouse where Thomas stayed was covered with water a foot deep. When another rain

FRINGED SNEEZEWEED
Helenium drummondii

RATTLEBUSH
Sesbania drummondii

came, a third of his plant collection rotted from the dampness and had to be thrown away.

As Thomas set out to explore further in the area, he had to travel by boat across wide prairies that were covered with more than nine feet of water. Thomas began to wonder if he would ever see dry land. Actually he worried more about the fact that his papers for pressing plants might never dry out again.

At Bell's Landing he saw dry land at last. Walking by the side of a rented ox cart that carried his luggage, Thomas finally collected enough specimens around San Felipe to make a shipment to Britain. So far he had gathered and packed 320 species of plants, seeds, roots, bulbs, and fruits, as well as bottles of snakes, lizards, and a horned lizard.

Although he had hoped to go further inland to the mountains, Thomas changed his plans. Indian attacks in the area made him decide to go to the seacoast. After a trip to hunt birds on Galveston Island during the winter and spring months of 1834–35, Thomas headed back to the mainland. Paddling an old canoe, he went up the coast more than one hundred miles by himself. Due to crop failures that year, food was so scarce that Thomas had many hungry days. He was often disheart-

RAIN-LILY
Zephyranthes drummondii

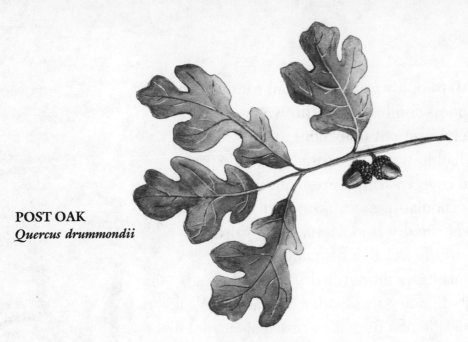

POST OAK
Quercus drummondii

ened and lonely since he did not know any other naturalists in Texas who might be interested in his experiences or collections.

For some weeks Thomas collected specimens around Gonzales and Fort Tenochtitlan (near the present town of Caldwell). For a change he was not bitten by mosquitoes. Due to the farmers' custom of burning off the prairies in late summer, there were not many insects to be found. But Thomas became so ill from the hot sun that he could not work for three months. However, by that time he had collected 750 species of plants and 150 species of birds.

It was time for Thomas Drummond to go home to Scotland. Even though he had had many difficulties, he planned to bring his wife and family back to settle in Texas. He believed he would be able to work for the Mexican government, which was looking for a naturalist to study plants and animals from eastern Mexico and Texas west to the Pacific Ocean. For this work he hoped to be paid with a grant of land. In a letter to a friend, Thomas wrote, ". . . If I can add the purchase of

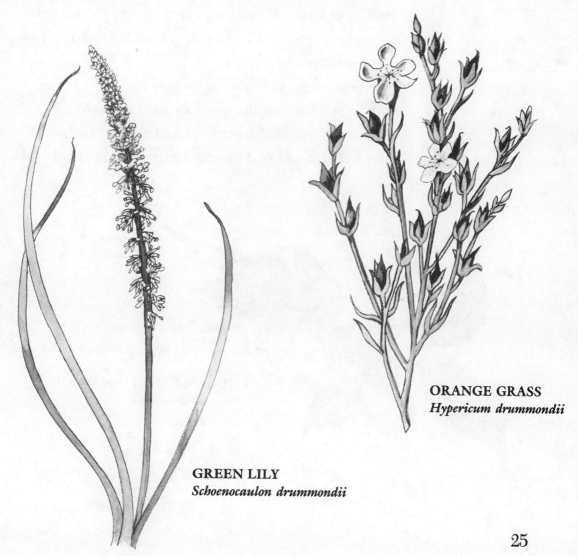

GREEN LILY
Schoenocaulon drummondii

ORANGE GRASS
Hypericum drummondii

a dozen cows and calves, which would cost ten dollars each (that is, the cow and calf) . . . my fortune would be made." He also thought he could earn a living by writing and selling a complete catalog of all the plants he had discovered.

None of these plans worked out. On his way back to Britain in 1835, Thomas sailed on a ship that stopped in Cuba for several days. He set out to make a quick collecting trip on the island during the stopover.

No one knows what happened after this. The only word his family ever received came in the mail from the British consul in Havana, Cuba. It was a certificate of Thomas Drummond's death.

ROUGH-LEAFED DOGWOOD
Cornus drummondii

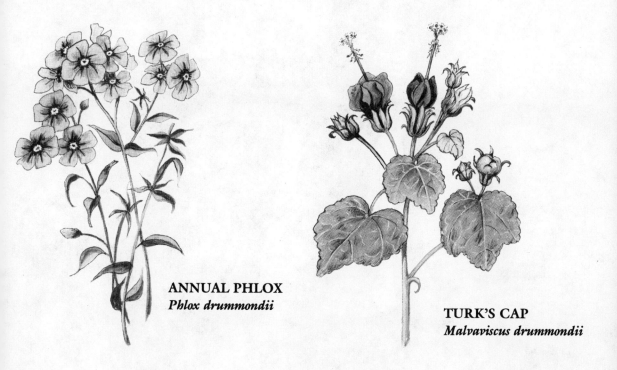

ANNUAL PHLOX
Phlox drummondii

TURK'S CAP
Malvaviscus drummondii

His friends had saved Thomas's letters and reports about his travels. They put them in the library at the Royal Botany Gardens in Kew, England, so that anyone who wished would be able to read them. Botanists named a number of new species of plants in honor of their good friend Thomas Drummond and sent specimens of his plants to museums throughout the world. In the Latin titles of plants, his name is seen many, many times.

And in England a lovely blue phlox is grown in memory of Thomas Drummond.

Areas where Drummond made his collections.

27

Ferdinand Jacob Lindheimer

Father of Texas Botany
1801–1879

GOAT'S RUE
Tephrosia lindheimeri

Most of the time Ferdinand Lindheimer was perfectly happy as a professor at a school in Frankfort, Germany. At school he could do what he liked best—which was to study about everything under the sun. He especially liked law, mathematics, all the sciences, and arts and languages.

It would have been a fine life in Germany if Ferdinand had not talked so loudly about the things he did *not* like. He told everyone within earshot that he did not like the way King Frederick Wilhelm III was keeping himself rich and everyone else poor. The king forced men to be in the army and to fight wars they did not believe in. He would not let people make up their own minds about what type of work they wanted to do. Ferdinand spoke out against these things until King Wilhelm finally heard him. The young professor was about to be put in prison along with some other loud talkers when he decided it would be wise to get on a ship going far, far away to America.

The year was 1833. After visiting with some German friends who had settled in Belleville, Illinois, young Ferdinand headed for Mexico. Once there, he had no trouble getting a job. When the owner of a banana and pineapple plantation found out how much the young German knew about plants, he hired Ferdinand on the spot. The planter even said that if Ferdinand cared to make any collections, he could have all the insects and plants he wanted. For the next sixteen months Ferdinand worked on the plantation and collected plants and insects to study in his spare time.

While in Mexico, Ferdinand heard that Mexican general Santa Anna had led soldiers to Texas to force the people there to obey him. This made Ferdinand furious. Nothing mattered more to him than freedom, especially since he had come to

IRON WEED
Vernonia lindheimeri

30

this new land to find it. He left his job immediately to go help the Texans fight.

As it turned out, he did not do any fighting, but luckily he knew how to swim. The sailing ship that carried him was wrecked in the Gulf of Mexico just off the coast of Alabama. Ferdinand had to swim ashore. Then he hurried on to Texas.

The day before Ferdinand reached Texas, the Texans won the war at the Battle of San Jacinto, and Santa Anna was captured. Texas was free from Mexico, and most of the great excitement was over.

Ferdinand stayed in Texas anyway. After traveling awhile, he tried farming near Houston for two years, but his heart was not in it. His real inter-

SENNA
Cassia lindheimeriana

TEXAS PRICKLY PEAR
Opuntia lindheimeri

31

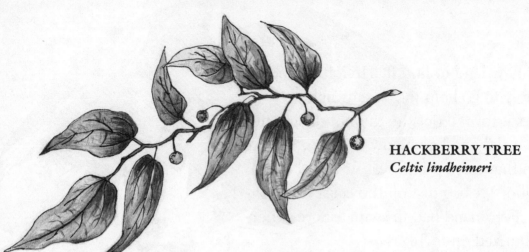

HACKBERRY TREE
Celtis lindheimeri

est, he decided, was in botany, and he wanted to explore for plants in the Texas wilderness. A friend suggested to Ferdinand that he write a letter to Dr. Asa Gray, a naturalist teaching at Harvard University in Massachusetts. Perhaps Dr. Gray would want someone to gather and classify plants in the new Republic of Texas. It so happened that Asa Gray was looking for just such a person, and he was glad to give the job to someone already in Texas, especially someone as knowledgeable as Ferdinand Lindheimer.

Ferdinand immediately bought a horse, two spotted hunting dogs, and a two-wheeled cart with a canvas top. Into the cart he packed flour, coffee, salt, a rifle, and a large pack of pressing papers made of silk tissues. Going off by himself with his dogs, horse, and cart, he walked all over Galveston Island, Houston, and the East Texas counties of Waller, Washington, Austin, and Colorado. During the trip he preserved hundreds of plants by drying and pressing them between the silk tissues. After he returned home, he packed his specimens carefully in wooden crates and sent them to Asa Gray at Harvard University.

Dr. Gray was glad to receive the plants so that he could write articles about the new species. He paid Ferdinand for his work and asked him to send more, and that is just what Ferdinand did for the next ten years. He collected and preserved many species of plants from the Houston, San Felipe, Cat Springs, and Victoria areas. In addition to mailing collections to Harvard, he sent many dried plants and much information to George Engelmann, a botanist at the Botanical Gardens in St. Louis, Missouri.

In December of 1844 Ferdinand was given a different job. A group of colonists from Germany landed in Texas. They needed a guide to show them to the land they had purchased on the Guadalupe River in Central Texas. Since Ferdinand knew how to talk with Indians and how to find his way in the wilderness where there were no roads, he was hired to take the new settlers to their land. After meeting them at the town of Velasco on the coast, he led the way inland.

DEVIL'S SHOESTRING
Nolina lindheimeriana

33

TEXAS STAR
Lindheimera Texana

It was a long, dangerous trip, with ox carts carrying the belongings of the German families and their children. It was also a slow trip, because almost everyone had to walk the whole way. There was much illness, and many people died. More than forty children were left as orphans. But enough people survived to build the town of New Braunfels on the Comal and Guadalupe rivers.

For his work as a guide, Ferdinand was given a grant of land in the new town, on the banks of the Comal River. He built a large garden and alongside it a small cabin of timbers with walls of rocks, mud, and dried grasses.

As soon as his cabin was finished, Ferdinand went out into the hills to make more collections of wild plants. Dr. Gray and the other botanists at Harvard were so pleased to receive the new specimens that they named more than thirty of the new species of wildflowers after Ferdinand. His last name, Lindheimer, is found in the Latin names of these plants.

TEXAS RAT SNAKE
Elaphe obsoleta lindheimeri

BALSAM GOURD
Ibervillea lindheimeri

Ferdinand kept going farther into the wilderness, where only Indians lived. Often he was gone for months at a time all by himself. Indians secretly watched him from behind trees and bushes. After they decided he was a medicine man looking for plants, they left him alone. In fact they felt he was a friend and even protected him from unfriendly tribes and wild animals. As for Ferdinand, he went quietly about his work and bothered no one, either in the town or out in the woods—unless someone tried to push him around, of course.

A visitor from Germany who met the botanist at about this time described him in a book. He said that Ferdinand had deep-blue eyes and a thick black beard and that he wore a blue jacket, yellow buckskin trousers, and coarse farmers' shoes. Evidently Miss Eleanor Reinarz, a young German woman in New Braunfels, liked the way he looked, because she married him in 1846. After they had several children, Ferdinand had to build a larger cabin. It was right next to the old one that Mrs. Lindheimer kept to use as a kitchen.

Ferdinand earned a living by continuing to sell dried plants to universities and botanical gardens. In 1852 he began a new career. In one of the tiny rooms of his house on the Comal River, he printed the town's first newspaper—the *Neu Braunfelser Zeitung*. He wrote the articles in German and set the type by himself. As one

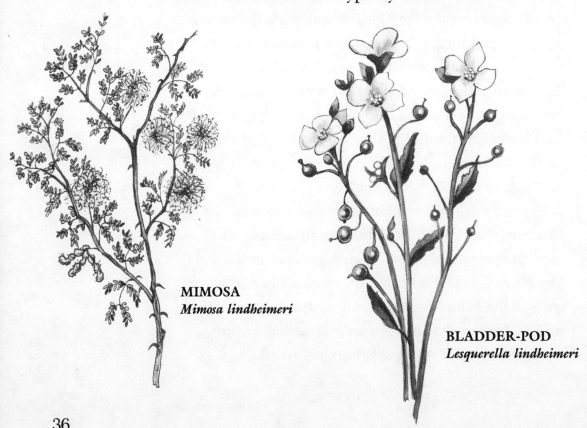

MIMOSA
Mimosa lindheimeri

BLADDER-POD
Lesquerella lindheimeri

might expect, Ferdinand wrote what he wanted to write even when the townspeople disagreed with him. Once some of his readers became so angered by an article that they picked up his printing press and threw it into the Comal River behind his house. But Ferdinand fished it out, carried it back to the house, and went right on printing.

During the Civil War, there was no paper available on which to print the news. What could Ferdinand use instead of paper? The precious supply of silk tissues came to mind. He had meant to save them for drying plants. But the war was of greater importance to the people, so Ferdinand printed the war news on the tissues. He wanted the German people of Texas to be aware of what was happening in the country where they lived.

Throughout his lifetime, many well-known visitors made their way to Lindheimer's home. For some months in the 1850's, the botanist Charles Wright taught in nearby San Marcos and gathered plants in the area. After he and Ferdinand met, they spent many hours exchanging information on the scientific discoveries of the times while sitting under the large trees in the Lindheimer front yard.

BEEBALM
Monarda lindheimeri

A famous naturalist from Germany, Dr. Ferdinand Roemer, also dropped in for chats with Lindheimer. He brought news from Germany, and together the two men took walks by the rivers and in the woods around New Braunfels.

Indians befriended by Ferdinand during his explorations continued to come see him. The Comanche chief Satanta arrived one day on his horse to find Lindheimer's young son playing in the yard. Satanta was captivated by the little boy's blond hair. It was a sight that Indians seldom saw, and they believed blond hair to be a symbol of good fortune. Satanta rode away and soon re-

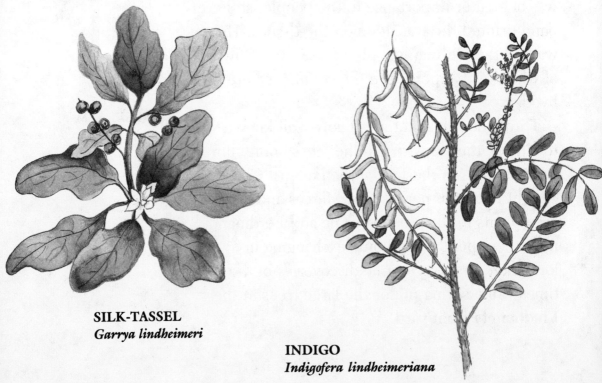

SILK-TASSEL
Garrya lindheimeri

INDIGO
Indigofera lindheimeriana

WHITE GAURA
Gaura lindheimeri

turned leading two mules and a little Mexican
girl. To Ferdinand, Satanta said, "You take mules
and little Mexican girl. Boy go with me." When
Ferdinand recovered from his astonishment, he
assured Satanta that he was not interested in such
a trade, and Satanta sadly rode away.

Ferdinand Lindheimer's long black beard
turned snowy white when he was an old man.
His blue eyes still sparkled as he talked about
the plants he was studying around New
Braunfels. And whenever school children
needed help with Latin or mathematics or any
other subject, they knocked on the door of the
little house on the Comal River. They were quite
certain that Ferdinand Lindheimer could tell
them something about everything under the sun.

*Areas where Lindheimer
made his collections.*

Charles Wright
1811–1885

CACTUS
Mammillaria wrightii

It was a good thing Charles Wright liked to walk. Otherwise he might never have become a naturalist. When he was a little boy, he rambled around every day in the woods near his home in Wethersfield, Connecticut. Not even deep snow in the wintertime could keep him from his walks.

By the time he went off to college at Yale University, he thought nothing of walking fifty miles over snowy roads to get home for Christmas vacations. Because his legs were quite short, it took him several days to go that far.

No one expected Charles to be a good student. He had had trouble with weak eyes all his life, but he did not let that stop him from excelling in Greek, Latin, mathematics, and all the sciences.

PALM BORER
Dinapate wrightii

As one might guess, Charles was painfully shy because of his weak eyes and short legs. When all the other students were going to school parties, Charles was off by himself, roaming the woods around the college grounds. Maybe at such times he first became interested in collecting plants.

Shyness, weak eyes, short legs—none of these things kept Charles from becoming one of the most outstanding naturalists in the world. During his lifetime he traveled thousands of miles, discovering new species of plants and insects in the United States, South Africa, Cuba, Japan, Central America, and of course Texas.

First he graduated with honors from Yale University in New Haven, Connecticut. From there he went to Natchez, Mississippi, to work as a tutor to the children of a wealthy plantation

GROUND CHERRY
Physalis wrightii

42

JIMSON WEED
Datura wrightii

owner. The job lasted only one year. During a depression when no one bought cotton, the plantation owner had no money to pay his tutor's salary. Now Charles headed west to the Republic of Texas, which had just won its freedom from Mexico.

The year was 1837. Charles was 26 years old. Since the Republic of Texas was just one year old, there was much to be done to make the new country more livable. For one thing, everyone who bought land needed to know exactly where the edges of his property met those of his neighbors. Charles worked as a surveyor to measure the land bought by the new settlers.

GOLDENROD
Solidago wrightii

CUDWEED
Gnaphalium wrightii

Surveying meant doing lots of walking again. It also meant that Charles's shoes were forever wearing out. There were no shoemakers around, so Charles learned how to make moccasins as the Indians did, from deer and buffalo hides. He also made leather leggings to protect his trousers from brambles and thorns.

One good thing about walking around the country making surveys was that Charles could collect plants at the same time. Becoming enthused by the great variety of plants in Texas, he gathered hundreds of wildflower and tree leaf specimens to press between papers to dry and preserve them.

At first Charles was much too busy to think about selling the plants he was collecting and preserving. To add to his earnings as a surveyor, he had begun to teach school in Zavala, a small town near the Louisiana border. It was all he could do to survive in that territory where horse thieves, gamblers, and rough desperadoes roamed.

As soon as he could, Charles moved to the more peaceful town of Columbus on the Colorado River. There was even a small college nearby at Rutersville—the first college in the Republic of Texas. Charles was hired as a professor at Rutersville College. Not only did he teach every-

thing from mathematics and surveying to Latin
and elocution, he also had to keep an eye out for
Indians, who often raided the area to steal horses.
Yet in spite of being overloaded with work,
Charles wrote to Dr. Asa Gray, a botany teacher
at Harvard University. He asked if he could collect Texas plants for him. Soon Charles was being
paid by Dr. Gray to send a constant supply of
new plants to the Harvard Museum.

After Rutersville College closed in 1846,
Charles worked as a tutor for private families.
In 1848 he went to Austin, where he taught
classes in a private school and made
botanical collections in the hills around
the town that had become the capital
of Texas.

BIRD'S BEAK
Cordylanthus wrightii

VERBENA
Verbena wrightii

BROWN FOOT
Perezia wrightii

An opportunity soon came for Charles to travel as a surveyor and botanist with a troop of soldiers being sent to guard the Texas-Mexico border. In Eagle Pass he made large collections of plants on each side of the Rio Grande and sent them to Harvard.

After three months in Eagle Pass, Charles had had enough of walking. That same year, 1848, he hurried back up north to accept a job in the herbarium at Harvard University near Boston. However, almost as soon as Charles had begun sorting plants for the herbarium, Asa Gray asked him to go back to Texas. Dr. Gray had heard that a group of soldiers were going to survey land for a road to be built from Austin to El Paso, a distance of 673 miles. He thought it would be a fine idea

STAR-VIOLET
Houstonia wrightii

DEER VETCH
Lotus wrightii

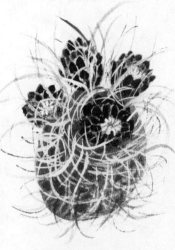

HEDGEHOG
Ferocactus wrightii

if Charles were to go along with the soldiers to make collections, because no one had ever studied the plants or insects in that part of Texas. And while Charles was at it, said Asa, he could help with surveying for the new road.

There was one trouble with Asa's fine plan. Once Charles was back in Texas, he found that the soldiers would carry only his trunk and drying papers in their wagons. There was no room for him! When he complained, the soldiers said they were only following their orders, and they were not going to disobey them for the likes of a little short-legged botanist. If Charles wanted to go, he would have to get his own horse, they said. Since

TACK STEM
Calycoseris wrightii

Charles had no money to buy a horse, he *walked* behind the wagons to El Paso—all 673 miles.

The men and wagons started west in June 1849. In 104 days they crossed the plains. All the while, Charles was making a huge collection of more than 570 specimens that included plants, animals, and insects. Even while the wagons were stuck during heavy rains, he discovered all sorts of unusual aquatic species of insects in the mud. Naturally, the soldiers thought he was a bit more than crazy to be poking around in the mud looking for bugs.

During three months of traveling, Charles suffered from either cold or burning heat, driving rains, bitter drinking water, hordes of flies, sore feet, and all too often not enough food. Even so, he gathered enough cacti and seeds of wild plants

to send 1,400 species to Harvard. His friend Asa
Gray wrote a special book about the findings. Its
title was in Latin—*Plantae Wrightianae*. In it Dr.
Gray described all the plants Charles Wright had
found in Texas, the places where he had found
them, and on what day. He also made Charles's
last name a part of each new plant's name.

By this time Charles had returned to teach
classes in San Marcos, Texas, and to gather
mosses and lichens in the area. He met the
scholarly Ferdinand Lindheimer at nearby New

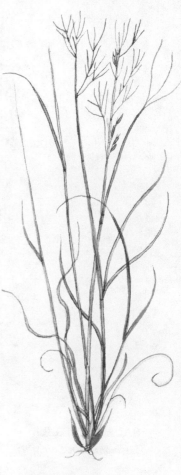

THREE AWN GRASS
Aristida wrightii

WILD BUCKWHEAT
Eriogonum wrightii

49

Braunfels and spent many hours with him. They often sat in the front yard of Lindheimer's home on the Comal River and talked about the discoveries being made in botany and other sciences.

Charles Wright went on one more trip as a botanist in Texas, with a group of men who were appointed to a boundary commission. They were asked to determine the boundary line between Mexico and the United States from the Rio Grande to the Pacific Ocean. Charles went along as a surveyor and botanist. He made a collection of a great many cacti in Texas, Arizona, and New Mexico to carry back to Harvard University. The journey was his last in the Southwest.

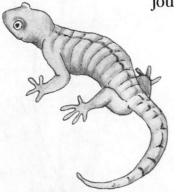

SALAMANDER
Desmognathus wrighti

MALLOW
Abutilon wrightii

GRAY FLYCATCHER
Empidonax wrightii

One would think Charles might have had his fill of walking by now. Actually he was just getting started. For the next sixteen years he made collections of plants in Australia, Hong Kong, Japan, Africa, Cuba, and elsewhere—every time he had the chance.

In 1868 he did not do quite so much walking after he became curator of the herbarium at Harvard. He stayed there seven years and then worked one year as a librarian on the campus.

For the last ten years of his life, Charles retired to his boyhood home in Wethersfield, Connecticut. Every day he walked over his farm and worked in his garden. In 1885 his life ended peacefully in a way that seemed most fitting— he was out walking in his lovely garden.

Areas where Wright made his collections.

51

John James Audubon
1785–1851

CEDAR WAXWING
Bombycilla cedrorum

Of all the naturalists who came to Texas, John James Audubon would turn out to be the most famous. He was also the one who had the most failures. During the first part of his life, it seemed as though he could not succeed at anything.

His father, a French sea captain, was quite sure that John James would grow up to be either a fine soldier or a brilliant engineer. In Santo Domingo (now the island of Haiti), where John James was born, there were no schools; so Captain Audubon took his son to France. There he sent him to the best of schools.

Instead of going to classes, John James went into the woods each day to look for birds, mosses, and nests with eggs in them. By the time he was ten, he had a room full of bird nests—and nothing but failing grades on his report cards.

Later, after John James failed tests in a military school, Captain Audubon sent his eighteen-year-old son to America to give him some business experience. The captain bought Mill Grove, a large estate near Philadelphia, so that John James would have a place in which to study farming and the lead mining business.

John James did not learn much about farming or lead mining, but he did find out a great deal about the animals in the woods on the estate. He filled the whole third floor of his house with stuffed squirrels, raccoons, possum, fish, frogs, snakes, lizards, and bird nests.

And when he was not hunting or sketching, he was either ice-skating, dancing, fencing, or playing the flute or violin. Besides, he had met Lucy

COLLARED PECCARY
Tayassu tajacu

SCISSOR-TAILED FLYCATCHER
Muscivora forficata

Bakewell, a young, pretty neighbor. A growing fondness for Lucy made it harder than ever for John James to keep his mind on being a businessman.

Not that John James did not try to do as his father wished. He tried to have a mining business with his friend Ferdinand Rozier. When that failed, he sold Mill Grove and went to work for Lucy's uncle in New York City. The office where he worked was located on the New York harbor. The trouble was that John James spent most of his time looking out the window, making drawings of the graceful seabirds that swooped over the harbor. One day, after he absentmindedly mailed an

CARDINAL
Richmondena cardinalis

MOCKINGBIRD
Mimus polyglottos

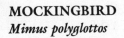

unsealed envelope containing $8,000 of the company's money, Lucy's uncle fired him without further ado.

Soon afterwards, John James and Rozier opened a general store in Louisville, Kentucky. At first the store did well. Lucy agreed to marry John James, and in 1809 she came to live in Louisville.

Many people came to the store just to watch John James draw pictures of birds and do card tricks. Even Rozier said that John James was the most likable fellow he ever knew. But John James went into the woods so often that Rozier seldom saw him. One time he disappeared for three days. While following and sketching a hawk, he had forgotten to watch the time.

Another day John James found a large hollow sycamore tree where a flock of swallows lived. In the evening he counted nine thousand birds flying into the tree in a half-hour's time. Naturally, he spent the night there so that he could hear the great roar of wings as the huge army of swallows left the tree early in the morning.

Fortunately, Lucy was an understanding wife. She knew that birds were important to her husband. She even said that she would take his place in the store to support their new son, Victor, so that John James could spend his time sketching. Lucy seemed to understand that no one else had ever drawn birds so perfectly, with every feather

BIGHORN SHEEP
Ovis canadensis auduboni

exactly the right shape, size, and color. No one but her husband could draw a bird that looked as though it might fly right off the page.

With Lucy's blessing, John James left home carrying on his back a blanket, a knapsack, food, water, a hunting knife, and on his shoulder a leather portfolio filled with drawing papers. On a boat going down the Ohio and Mississippi rivers, he sketched birds sighted during the day. At night he played the flute and danced Irish jigs to entertain the boat passengers and drew pictures of them to pay for his fare.

When John James returned home some months later, he put two hundred drawings in a rawhide trunk for safekeeping. Then he started another store in Ste. Genevieve, Missouri, with Rozier. After a few months he left to walk 165 miles back

TEXAS ARMADILLO
Dasypus novemcinctus

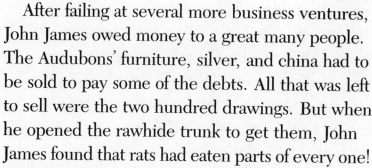

DESERT COTTONTAIL
Sylvilagus audubonii

to Kentucky to see his second young son, John Woodhouse Audubon. Thus ended his partnership with Rozier.

After failing at several more business ventures, John James owed money to a great many people. The Audubons' furniture, silver, and china had to be sold to pay some of the debts. All that was left to sell were the two hundred drawings. But when he opened the rawhide trunk to get them, John James found that rats had eaten parts of every one!

The sheriff in Louisville put him in jail for not paying all of his debts. To pass the time, John James drew birds on the walls of the jail. He also made an important decision. He promised himself that he would never again try to be a businessman; instead he would be an artist. He would travel across America, draw all the birds he saw, and publish his work in a book. And each drawing would be the actual size of each bird, even if the bird were six feet tall!

WOOD WARBLER
Dendroica auduboni

After John James was released from jail, Lucy agreed to support their two boys by teaching while her husband traveled and drew birds in the South. Wherever he went, he made his living doing chalk portraits and teaching classes in dancing, music, drawing, and fencing. In any spare time he worked at redoing the drawings the rats had eaten. When one hand grew tired, John James used the other. He needed both hands, for he drew incessantly, rising at three o'clock every morning and working far into the night.

By 1826 John James felt that he had made enough drawings and paintings for a book. When he took his work to American publishers, they thought his drawings were the finest they had ever seen. However, they were horrified when John James insisted that the drawings be printed as large as he had drawn them. "No one has ever made such a big book," they shouted. "Who would turn pages that were four feet high?"

Not one to be easily discouraged, John James boarded a sailing ship to England with his precious portfolio of 240 bird paintings. There he found engravers who were willing to publish his work in full size. John James wrote the scientific details for the book with the help of William MacGillivray, a Scottish naturalist. Writing a description of the birds in each picture took them two years.

The engravings of the life-size paintings were each colored by hand. Eventually there were enough bird paintings, 435 of them, to make 4 volumes. Each volume weighed 50 pounds and had pages 5 feet square. Because the pages, called folios, were large and heavy, people referred to the paintings as "Elephant Folios."

Entitled *Birds of America*, the great volumes were an instant success. Even the King of England, George IV, subscribed to a set. John James became a celebrity overnight. In London crowds of people followed him as he walked along the

WHOOPING CRANE
Grus Americana

streets carrying the heavy portfolio of paintings on his shoulder. Because he wore a wolfskin coat, long flowing hair, and floppy trousers, the English people called him "The American Woodsman."

By the time he returned to America in 1831, John James had become a famous and wealthy man. He stayed famous, but he did not stay wealthy for long. Almost immediately he began to make more trips and more paintings for another book. A great deal of time and money were needed for traveling and for preparing new volumes that would depict American quadrupeds (four-legged animals) as well as more birds. His two sons took painting lessons so they could work with him. Victor learned to paint landscapes for backgrounds, and John Woodhouse excelled in drawing animals.

In 1837 during April and May, John James came to Texas. "I am going to search for new species and examine the habits of birds," he said.

BLACKFOOTED FERRET
Mustela nigripes

COYOTE
Canis latrans

For three weeks on Galveston Island, he explored the bayous and harbors, where he found more species of birds and animals than he had ever seen—and also more mosquitoes. On the linen pages of his journal, he wrote that "two-thirds of all the species in the United States occur in Texas." Blue-winged teal, snowy and blue heron, sandpipers, black-necked stilts, gulls, terns, hawks, widgeons, spoonbills, and ducks were just a few of the varieties he saw. His most unusual discovery, he said, was a "rattlesnake with double re-curved fangs, which, I am told, will prove a new genus." He was also the first naturalist to claim that not only could snakes climb trees but they also ate bird eggs. Scientists laughed at him and said he was wrong. But years later his observation was proven correct.

On May 18, 1837, John James and his friends rowed twelve miles over a rain-filled bayou to the city of Houston. Determined to meet Sam Houston, president of the new Republic of Texas, they waded down the streets through water above their ankles to get to the president's home, a small log cabin of two mud-caked rooms. There John James visited with the tall, scowling Sam Houston and his cabinet members while Indians and horses sloshed through the soggy streets outside.

RACCOON
Procyon lotor

GREAT-HORNED OWL
Bubo Virginianus

AUDUBON'S ORIOLE
Icterus gradua cauda

Along Buffalo Bayou in Houston, John James saw hundreds of ivory-billed woodpeckers. In fact he said he saw birds in such great numbers and varieties that they surpassed all "the mass of observation in ornithology (the study of birds)." Well satisfied, he returned home to Pennsylvania.

While in Texas, John James painted four quadrupeds—the cotton rat, the collared peccary, the Texan skunk, and the black-tailed hare. Some years later, in 1845, he sent his son John Woodhouse to Texas to look for animals around Castroville, La Grange, Corpus Christi, and San Antonio. John Woodhouse mailed the skins of animals back to his father after preserving them in rum. When John James received them, he wired the skins into realistic positions in order to make his paintings of them as lifelike as possible for a new book on quadrupeds.

After one more lengthy trip to explore the Midwest in 1843, John James settled in the state of New York. He bought 24 acres on the Hudson River and built a large house, which he gave to his faithful wife. He wanted to honor her for all her years of labor in helping him with his work. Because John James had never learned to write well in English, Lucy had rewritten everything he ever wrote so that his use of the language would be correct.

When the Audubons were not entertaining distinguished visitors from all over the world, they were working on the books about quadrupeds. After John James began to lose his eyesight, Lucy and their sons and friends finished the work. Called *Quadrupeds of America*, the books were published by a Philadelphia engraver, with the last of four volumes appearing in 1854, three years after John James's death.

Areas where Audubon made his collections.

The Audubon paintings were so successful that they are still being printed today, more than 150 years later. The works of John James Audubon, the man who had failed so many times, won far greater success and recognition than the dedicated artist-naturalist ever dreamed of. Today his paintings and books are held as treasures in museums and private collections all over the world.

Ferdinand Roemer
1818–1891

RED CEDAR SAGE
Salvia roemeriana

No one who ever saw Dr. Ferdinand Roemer could forget him. He was a very large man who laughed a lot and dressed in wrinkled, shabby clothes. And he ate heaping platefuls of food even though he had not a tooth in his head. Being toothless did not keep him from talking a great deal. In fact the only times he was not talking were when he was eating, sleeping, or smoking his long black cigars.

If no one was nearby, Dr. Ferdinand (as everyone called him) either talked to himself or wrote about all of the interesting ideas in his head. But much of the time there were people gathered around to hear the jokes he told about himself and his adventures.

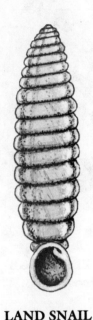

LAND SNAIL
Holospira roemeri

Dr. Ferdinand was like a book, one of his friends said, because he was full of good answers to all kinds of questions. He especially liked questions about the land and mountains in Germany, the country where he was born. After earning a doctorate degree from the University of Berlin, Dr. Ferdinand made a study of the mountains along the Rhine River. In 1844 he wrote a book about these geological formations. When it was published, it became one of the best-known books in all of Germany.

There were more than enough mountains in Germany to keep Dr. Ferdinand studying and writing for the rest of his life. But one day a letter came to Berlin University from the new Republic of Texas, far off in North America. The letter was from Solms-Braunfels, a prince who had led a shipload of families from Germany to settle in Texas. Prince Solms wrote that he suspected there might be silver and other precious metals in Central Texas where the Germans were making their homes. It would be most helpful, he said, if the university would send a trained geologist, someone who could tell by studying the soil and rocks just where to look for the precious metals.

Dr. Ferdinand's friends saw that he was the best man for the job and encouraged him to go.

The Berlin Academy promised to pay his way if he would send back geological information and specimens of plants and animals.

After Dr. Ferdinand chewed on his cigar awhile, he agreed to explore the land in Central Texas, even though it was full of Indians and wild animals.

In 1845, when he was 27 years old, Dr. Ferdinand sailed to America. Landing on the island of Galveston, he spent seven weeks collecting plants and animals from the land and sea. Large numbers of crabs, mussels, jellyfish, sea urchins, and a horned lizard were shipped back to the Academy of Science in Berlin.

Dr. Ferdinand kept track of all the things he saw by writing about them in a journal. A good speller, he easily wrote the long scientific names in Latin, such as *Pelecanus americanus* (long-billed pelican); Phrynosoma orbula reseavigm (horned lizard); and Celtis crassifolai Lam (hackberry tree). He also wrote that he had found a huge mound of Gnathodon cuneatus Gray (mussels).

Not many people in Texas could understand what Dr. Ferdinand had written, but in Germany scientists were elated to receive all the scientific information he sent back.

SPURGE
Tithymalis roemerianus

When Dr. Ferdinand went to Houston in January 1846, he found a room in the Capitol Hotel. The hotel was quite shabby and had a leaking roof. However, since it was the only hotel in town, Dr. Ferdinand decided it was better than a tent.

Gathered in the lobby around the hotel's black iron stove was a crowd of men who talked all night long. The men were eager to tell Dr. Ferdinand the news that Texas had just become part of the United States. In the capital city of Austin, President Anson Jones had taken down the flag of the Republic of Texas and raised the Stars and Stripes with Texas as the twenty-eighth star.

STRAWBERRY CACTUS
Cereus roemeri

Caught up in the excitement, Dr. Ferdinand stayed up most of the night listening, talking, and chewing on his cigar. When he finally went to bed, he discovered several strangers asleep in his room—all of them snoring. In this way he found out that Texas travelers had to share scarce hotel rooms with anyone who came along. But by that time Dr. Ferdinand was too sleepy to mind.

In a few days he met Nicholas Zink, a merchant who was setting out for the German settlement of New Braunfels in Central Texas. As this was exactly where he wanted to go, Dr. Ferdinand asked if he could make the trip with Mr. Zink.

"There's no room in my two wagons. They're filled with baggage, people, and cotton goods," said Mr. Zink. "But if you'll acquire your own horse, you're welcome to come along."

Traveling with a wagon train was safer than riding all the way alone. Even though he was not much of a horseman, Dr. Ferdinand gladly bought a horse for the trip. His purchase paid off, because heavy rains caused the wagons to sink in the mud twenty times. If Dr. Ferdinand, his horse, and the other travelers had not pulled the wagons out of the mud all twenty times, they might be there yet.

At night the travelers slept under the wagons

MIMOSA
Schrankia roemeriana

71

to keep out of the rain. Without dry wood to make cooking fires at mealtimes, Dr. Ferdinand and the others ate cold bacon and raw sweet potatoes.

Dr. Ferdinand made a fine story out of the trip. He wrote about the rivers, creeks, rocks, shrubs, and Tillandsia usneoides L. (Spanish moss) that hung from trees like a grey curtain. He declared that the tallest trees were the *Plantanus occidentalis L.* and the *Populus angulata Ait.* Of course, Mr. Zink and the other travelers would have called them "sycamores" and "cottonwoods."

Passing through San Felipe, the travelers saw only six log houses—all that remained of the large, prosperous village started by Stephen F. Austin. San Felipe had been burned ten years earlier during the war with Mexico, and no one had come back to rebuild the homes and shops.

It took seventeen days to travel 190 miles from Houston to New Braunfels. As usual, Dr. Ferdinand was quite hungry when he arrived. The first thing he did was find a boarding house where hearty German-style meals were served three times a day.

The second thing Dr. Ferdinand did was visit some friendly Lipan Indians who were moving their camp across the Guadalupe River. He

GOLD-EYE PHLOX
Phlox roemeriana

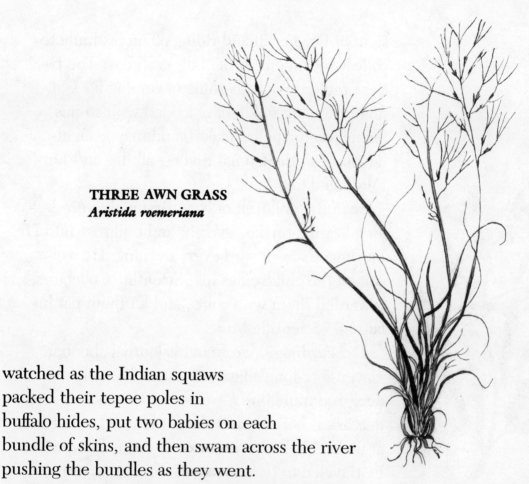

THREE AWN GRASS
Aristida roemeriana

watched as the Indian squaws
packed their tepee poles in
buffalo hides, put two babies on each
bundle of skins, and then swam across the river
pushing the bundles as they went.

    The third thing Dr. Ferdinand did was look up
the well-known botanist Ferdinand Lindheimer.
The two Ferdinands explored the land around
New Braunfels and declared the clear, sparkling
springs and rivers the most beautiful they had
ever seen.

    One of the wisest things Dr. Ferdinand did was
buy a mule. Townfolk became familiar with the

sight of Dr. Ferdinand riding off on his mule to collect specimens in the hills each day. The patient mule thought nothing of coming back at night carrying saddlebags loaded with stones, plants, cacti, shells, snakes, and maybe an alligator from the Comal River—all this and Dr. Ferdinand too!

Soon the children of New Braunfels were lugging lizards, turtles, garfish, and bullfrogs into Dr. Ferdinand's front yard every evening. He welcomed the children as his "Scientific Collectors," rewarded them with coins, and let them pat his faithful "Scientific Mule."

Dr. Ferdinand wrote in his journal about an eleven-foot-long alligator in Comal Creek, about deer, hummingbirds, wolves, ocelots, silver foxes, peccaries, herons, and about the cicadas that sang at night. He had even more to write about when he traveled to Bastrop, La Grange, and Torrey's Trading Post near Waco. At La Grange one night he was dazzled by a field full of glowworms. Near Waco he visited a village of Caddo Indians who were busy eating a fresh crop of watermelons when he arrived. They did not take time to talk with Dr. Ferdinand or listen to him either.

On his way back to New Braunfels, Dr. Ferdinand had to fight a prairie fire (which he acci-

TWO-LEAVED SENNA
Cassia roemeriana

dentally set while making coffee at his campsite).
Becoming ill, he had to send someone to find his
mule which had chewed through the tether-rope
one night and wandered off into the wilderness.

Shortly after Christmas in New Braunfels,
Dr. Ferdinand was at last able to take the long-
planned trip to the San Saba area north of the
Llano River to look for precious
metals. It so happened that
John O. Meusebach, leader
of the German colonists, was
going to the San Saba to make
a peace treaty with tribes of
Comanches. He invited
Dr. Ferdinand to go along to
make his scientific studies
of the land.

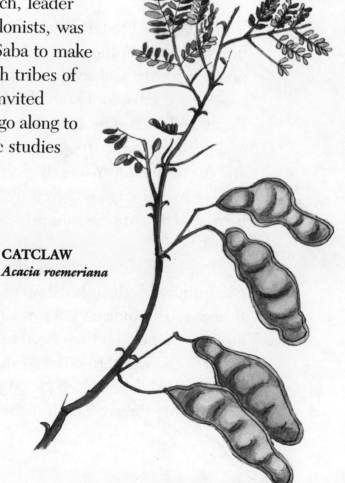

CATCLAW
Acacia roemeriana

CARBONACEOUS CHERT

LAND SNAIL
Mesodon roemeri

Heading for Fredericksburg, Dr. Ferdinand and the other men in the party filled wagons with presents for the Comanches—woolen goods, cotton, and tobacco. On the back of his mule, Dr. Ferdinand packed his own supplies—a rifle, several pistols, flour, coffee, salt, sugar, a tin cup, and two woolen blankets. Eight pack mules and three covered wagons driven by Mexican men carried more supplies and presents for the Indians.

After traveling for several days, the men saw two hundred Indians lined up on a hill in the distance. The Indians were mounted on horses, and the feathers on their heads and lances fluttered in the wind. In order to show that he came as a friend, John Meusebach emptied his rifle by firing it into the air. The Indians then rode to meet the white men and gathered with them for a peace council around a campfire.

After many hours of talking, the Indians and the white men signed a pact. Dr. Ferdinand sat with them on a circle of buffalo skins and took two puffs from the peace pipe, which was passed to each person. He listened as the Comanches agreed to allow the white men to settle in the area of the Llano River. In return, the Comanches were to receive 1,000 Spanish dollars and trading rights. Each side promised to allow the other to travel in safety.

To show that they meant to keep their promise, the Comanche warriors vigorously hugged Dr. Ferdinand and the other men. After serving a dinner of venison and rice, the Indians exchanged gifts with the white men and sang chants throughout the night.

For the next several days, Dr. Ferdinand traveled in the area making a detailed study of the land. He noted red granite at the Llano River, sandstone and feldspar, white quartz, and extremely rocky soil. He described in his journal the grey limestone hillsides, the fossils, sparse grass, and stunted oak trees. But nowhere did he find any signs of the silver deposits that had been reported. However, he wrote that there was black

CRUCIFIXION THORN
Juncus roemerianus

SHELL
Donax roemeriana

LAND SNAIL
Retinella roemeri

chert containing carbon in the soil, a sign that coal was present in the ground.

When the scientists in Germany received the report he mailed to them, it was the first news they had ever had about the geology of Central Texas. Dr. Ferdinand made it plain, however, that there was not much fertile soil for farming; nor were there enough forests for large lumber mills to prosper; and certainly no precious metals could be mined in that area.

His exploring mission over, Dr. Ferdinand returned to New Braunfels to pack his collection of rocks and plants for the return trip to Germany. On the day of his departure for the coast, Texas friends sadly gathered to bid him farewell. Climbing into the wagon to sit next to the driver, the doctor sat on the wooden seat, which promptly

broke with a loud crash. From the floor of the
wagon Dr. Ferdinand cheerily waved his hat and
cigar while hearty laughter broke out among the
Texans. It could be heard until the wagon went
out of sight down the road toward Seguin.

When Dr. Ferdinand returned to Germany,
the year was 1847. He taught in universities for
the rest of his life, gaining fame as a teacher and a
scientist. It came as no surprise to anyone when
he was elected to the Royal Scientific Societies of
Berlin, St. Petersburg, and Munich. Among the
250 works that he wrote were *Texas*, published in
1849, and *The Cretaceous Formations of Texas*,
published in 1852. Because he was the first naturalist to make a study of the rocks and soils, Dr.
Ferdinand is known today as "The Father of Texas
Geology."

*Areas where Roemer
made his collections.*

Gideon Lincecum
1793–1874

GRAPE
Vitis lincecomii

Just about the time the Lincecum family would settle in one place, Gideon's father would decide that cotton grew taller and grass grew greener somewhere else. He would load up the wagons and, with his wife, ten children, and all their belongings, rattle off through the wilderness looking for a new home. Before Gideon was a grown man, he had lived on plantations in Georgia, South Carolina, Mississippi, Alabama, and Tennessee.

At each stopping place, Gideon's best friends were the Indian children who lived in the area. From them he learned to shoot with a blow gun and to catch fish with barbed spears or a bow and arrow. The Indians taught him to speak their lan-

81

HONEY BEE
Apis mellifera

guages, to imitate bird calls, and to find plants that could be used for food or medicines.

"I was made for the forest," declared Gideon. "It's the place where I feel at home."

Although it saddened him to part with his Indian friends, Gideon, like his father, was eager to travel to new places. As the oldest son, he would run ahead of the wagons to hack a road through the forests. With bow and arrows, he and his brother shot deer and wild turkey for family suppers by the campfire. They climbed trees to look for honey, collected nuts, and gathered eggs from prairie hens that nested in the meadows. Not a tree, plant, bird, nor animal escaped their notice.

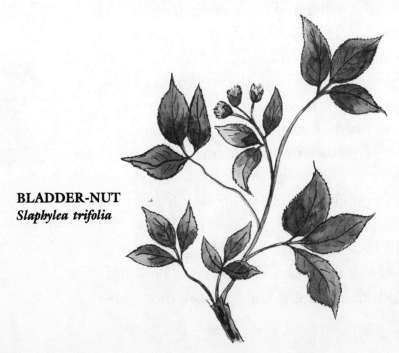

BLADDER-NUT
Slaphylea trifolia

Although Gideon learned to be a keen observer of forests and farmlands, he often wished he could read. However, his family owned no books, and their moving so often left Gideon no time for school.

An opportunity finally came when Gideon was fourteen. By then he was six feet tall, already a young man, with long black hair and blue eyes that sparkled under bushy eyebrows. In the small log schoolhouse near Eatonton, Georgia, the younger children knew far more about reading and writing than Gideon did. But in the five months of school that he attended, Gideon not only learned to read well and do arithmetic, he also memorized Webster's *Speller* all the way through.

Learning to read opened up a whole new world to Gideon. While working as a clerk at an Indian trading post, he was able to make use of a library of a thousand fine books left at the store by a traveler. Each day when his work was done, Gideon read the works of philosophers and scientists. "It was as though great floods of light came into my mind," he later said of that time.

Soon another precious gift came to Gideon. At dawn on Christmas Day, 1810, there was a knock on his door. Ichabod Thompson, owner of the

SIDEOATS GRAMA GRASS
Bouteloua curtipendula

83

trading post, was standing on the doorstep. In his hands Ichabod held a gift for his young clerk—a black violin made especially for him. In spite of the morning cold, barefooted Gideon joyfully stepped outside in his nightshirt and picked out his favorite melody on the new instrument. It was a Scottish tune called "Killiecrankie Is My Song." From that day on, the black violin was his constant companion. And each Christmas for the rest of his life, Gideon greeted the light of day by playing "Killiecrankie" three times over.

When he was twenty, Gideon married fourteen-year-old Sarah Bryant. They moved near the town of Columbus, Mississippi. For the next ten years Gideon worked in a mercantile store to support his growing family. His evenings were spent poring over books on medical subjects. When his friends found out how much he had learned about medicine, they asked him to practice as a doctor.

Gideon opened an office in town and rode his horse, Old Ned, to make house calls. Soon he was so popular as a doctor that he had to build a hospital near his home. Sarah fed the patients, and the Lincecum home was opened to the overflow of people who came with illnesses to be cured.

Unlike other doctors in the area, Gideon was a

RED CLOVER
Trefolium incarnatum

MONARCH BUTTERFLY
Danaus plexippus

botanic physician. After spending six weeks in the woods studying herbs with an Indian medicine man, Gideon was convinced that certain plants could be used safely to treat sick people. For medicines he made mixtures of various roots, leaves, barks, seeds, and flowers. He was not bothered by the fact that other doctors disapproved of his use of medicinal plants. His patients found his herbal remedies effective, and Gideon became a very successful doctor.

A new kind of excitement swept through Mississippi in 1834. Word came that Mexico was offering many acres of land to colonists who would make their homes in Texas, a vast territory held by Mexico. Interested people asked Gideon to go as a doctor with an expedition of men to explore Texas and bring back a report.

Nothing pleased Gideon more than setting out

SOAP GENTIAN
Gentiana saponaria

PEPPERMINT
Mentha piperita

west across the country on Old Ned. The little company of five men on horseback left Mississippi in January 1835. With two pack horses, a dog, some kettles, sacks of cornmeal, bacon, and a coffeepot, the men traveled for two months through East Texas. They saw thousands of deer, wild geese, and great herds of wild horses and buffalo. Only rarely did they see any houses or people. After a few weeks, all the men were ready to go home—that is, all but Gideon.

"I'm just getting started. I want to study the rivers and soils to see if the land is good for farming," he said to his friends. "You go on home without me."

Gideon set off on Old Ned with a pack horse, a tent, and a tin bucket. Camping each night, he ranged from the Gulf Coast to San Antonio and west to the site of present-day Fredericksburg. Along the coast he studied the mouths of the rivers and the kinds of plants that grew around them. All the while, he was collecting shells, fossils, birds, and grasses, and loading them on the pack horse. Crossing a river, Gideon would make a raft of cottonwood logs held together with a lacing of grape vines. These rafts would carry his belongings across the river while Old Ned swam alongside.

Near the Nueces River, Gideon was captured by Comanche Indians and taken to their camp. The Indians became friendlier when he spoke to them in the Choctaw language, which they could understand. Gideon made himself at home with the Comanches. He taught songs and dances to the children. He delighted the medicine man of the tribe by showing him his growing collection of medicinal plants.

However, several days later, Gideon saw a chance to escape. He told the Indians that he wanted to hunt for plants in order to make more medicines. They allowed him to leave camp. As soon as he was out of their sight, Gideon spurred Old Ned to his fastest gallop. For two days and nights Gideon and his horse did not stop for more

CICADA
Tibicen dorsata

JUNE BUG
Phyllophaga spp.

HAIRY SCORPION
Hadrurus arizonensis

than two minutes at a time. As they rushed by the trees and bushes, Old Ned grabbed leaves and branches to eat. At last, when he was sure they were not being followed, Gideon slowed Old Ned down to a leisurely walk through the wilderness.

Continuing to the east, Gideon explored the land between the Brazos and Colorado rivers. Eleven miles from Brenham, he came upon a high, grassy piece of land that was shaped like a long point. It overlooked Yegua Creek, which teemed with fish. The picturesque landscape and fertile land stayed in Gideon's mind long after he returned to his home and family in Mississippi. However, he took up his practice as a botanical doctor once again and became active in many organizations in the community of Columbus.

Twelve years later Gideon determined to move all of his family to Texas. Several of his children were married and had children of their own by then. They all went with him to Texas in 1847, just a year after Texas had become part of the United States. At Long Point, Gideon made homes for his family on 1,828 acres of land bought with gold he had saved. He called his plantation Mount Olympus. From the fertile black soil that was laced by many creeks, the Lincecum family

IRON-WEED
Vernonia noveloracensis

raised crops of corn, sugar cane, and grapes in abundance.

One year insects caused great damage to the crops. To save the harvest, Gideon and his children went down the rows picking off bugs from each plant. This experience spurred his interest in the study of insects and their habits. In fact Gideon, at age 68, decided to devote all of his time to the study of natural history. Having trained his five sons to be doctors, he felt that they could take his place to meet the medical needs of the community. He spent his days in the woods and fields observing ants, tarantulas, spiders, bees, butterflies, scorpions, horned lizards—everything that crossed his path.

For hours at a time Gideon knelt over ant hills, patiently watching the inhabitants as they scurried about. Over several years' time he learned their habits—how they ate, laid their eggs, built homes, and organized themselves into work units. He even found that some ants planted grasses near their hills so that they would be close to a food supply. Gideon named them Harvester Ants.

By writing numerous articles for *The American Naturalist,* a nature magazine, and letters to his friends about his findings, Gideon came to the attention of scholars at the Academy of Natural

TWO-SPOTTED LADY BUG
Adalia bipunctata

COTTON BOLL WEEVIL
Anthonomus grandis

HARVESTER ANT
Pogonomyrmex barbatus

INDIAN ROOT
Aralia racemosa

Sciences in Philadelphia. When botany professors and private collectors read of his observations, they realized that although Gideon had had little schooling, he had learned more about nature from his field studies than he would have from available books. Many of these people wrote to ask him to send specimens and information about insects and plants in Texas. To one collector in New York, Gideon sent two thousand butterflies. To the academy, and to scientists, professors, and other collectors, he sent thousands of plant and insect specimens.

Another interest that added to his daily work was a study of the weather. With a barometer ordered by mail, Gideon kept daily weather records of his home county of Washington and sent them to the Smithsonian Institution in Washington, D.C. He was delighted when the Smithsonian appointed him the official weather observer for his county. To newspapers in Texas

MUD DAUBER
Sceliphron caementarium

LUNA MOTH
Actias luna

he sent weather reports, positions of the stars, and advice on planting times.

Gideon's enthusiasm for nature was endless. Added to it was his love of people and making music. Each evening at his Long Point home, he brought out the black violin. With his daughter Sallie at the piano, he played duets to entertain the family and neighbors who gathered to listen and sing. His beloved wife, Sarah, embroidering as she sat in her rocking chair by the fireplace, was as happy as Gideon to be surrounded by their children and friends.

The Civil War years, 1861 to 1867, were devastating to the Lincecum plantation. Most of the men in the area went off to war, leaving no one to help with planting and harvesting crops. To make a living Gideon had to practice as a doctor again. Yet, as often as he could, he traveled across Texas to gather plants and insects. In 1867 he sent to the Smithsonian important collections he had

MILKWEED
Asclepias verticillata

made in eighteen counties. There were boxes and boxes of mammals, fossils, shells, birds, insects, and animal specimens in alcohol. More than one thousand plant specimens that he sent to a friend in Philadelphia were later given to the Herbarium in Paris, France.

Deeply upset by the Civil War, the ruin of his plantation, and the death of his wife in 1867, Gideon determined to start over in a new place. In 1868 he moved to Tuxpán, Mexico, with his widowed daughter Leonora and her children. With his usual vigor and enthusiasm, he worked hard to establish a farm and to discover what kinds of insects and plants surrounded his new home. All the while, he hoped the rest of his

BLACK-SNAKE ROOT
Sanicle marylandica

HORNED LIZARD
Phrynosoma cornutum

children and their families would come from
Texas to join him. And each morning he played
his violin before taking a swim in the river that
ran by his home.

Entertaining a host of friends among the
American colonists and the Mexican people in
Tuxpán, Gideon was happy. No one knows why
he suddenly left Mexico in June 1873. Perhaps it
was because he wanted to see his family and old
home at Long Point once again. Or perhaps he
wanted to gather nature specimens in Texas once
more, for he sent a collection—his last—to
the Smithsonian in 1874.

It is known that on the final Christmas of his
life, Gideon arose at dawn, stepped outside the
door in his nightshirt, and lifted the black violin
to his shoulder. And then the lively strains of
"Killiecrankie Is My Song" wafted over the woods
and meadows of Long Point for the last time.

*Areas where Lincecum
made his collections.*

93

TIME LINE

Texas belongs to Mexico   1821–1836

Jean Louis Berlandier

Thomas Drummond

Texas is a Republic   1836–1846

Ferdinand Jacob Lindheimer

Charles Wright

John James Audubon

Texas becomes part of the United States   1846

Ferdinand Roemer

Gideon Lincecum

94

1821 After belonging to Spain, Texas becomes part of Mexico when it gains its freedom from Spain.

300 families come from the United States to make the first Anglo settlement in Texas at San Felipe de Austin.

1828 Mexico sends a commission to set a boundary line between Louisiana and Texas. LOUIS BERLANDIER travels with the Boundary Commission to make a collection of plants and animals for European museums.

1833 THOMAS DRUMMOND of Scotland comes to collect Texas plants for his patron at the University of Glasgow.

1835 At Washington-on-the-Brazos, 59 men sign a Declaration of Independence from Mexico.

Dr. GIDEON LINCECUM makes his first trip to Texas.

1836 Texas gains freedom from the rule of Mexico at the Battle of San Jacinto and becomes a republic.

FERDINAND LINDHEIMER of Germany joins the Texan forces. Later, he makes a home in New Braunfels where he collects plants for botanical museums in the United States.

1837 CHARLES WRIGHT of Connecticut comes to Texas to teach and to collect plants and insects for Harvard University.

JOHN JAMES AUDUBON comes to Texas to paint birds and animals in preparation for several books.

1846 The Republic of Texas is dissolved when Texas joins the United States as the 28th state.

Dr. FERDINAND ROEMER is sent from Germany to study the geology of Central Texas. Landing in Galveston in 1845, he spends the next 16 months studying the land and making collections of plants and animals.

Dr. GIDEON LINCECUM of Mississippi settles near LaGrange, Texas. He spends his life making collections and field studies of plant and insect life, weather, and all aspects of nature.

1861 to 1865 Texas joins the Confederacy to fight the Civil War.

The first railroads, telegraph, and cattle drives mark the start of a new era for the state of Texas.

Five Who Also Came . . .

Edwin James
1797–1861

Dr. Edwin James of Vermont was the first trained American naturalist known to have made collections in the area of Texas. In 1820 he spent fifteen days in the Panhandle as a surgeon-naturalist to an expedition exploring the land and waterways between the Mississippi River and the Rocky Mountains. Dr. James kept the official records of the trip and made collections of plant and animal life along the Canadian River. These collections were sent to scientists in New York.

Jacob Boll
1828–1880

Born in Switzerland, Jacob Boll became a pharmacist and a collector of plants in Germany. He came to the Dallas area in 1869 to live and to make geological investigations. To Harvard University he sent more than fifteen thousand specimens of insects and all classes of animals. In the area around Wichita Falls, Texas, Boll was the first scientist to unearth fossil fish, reptiles, and amphibians. He discovered two hundred species new to science.

Gustaf Belfrage
1834–1882

Gustaf Belfrage was born in Stockholm, Sweden. He studied forestry and managed the forests of the Royal House before moving to Texas in 1867. Near Clifton and Norse, he gathered large collections of ants, glowworms, moths, beetles, butterflies, and other insects, sending them to the Swedish Academy of Science. Over fifteen years, he collected and sold 25,000 insect specimens, many of which are named for him. At the time of his death, he was in the process of preparing 36,881 pinned specimens.

Julien Reverchon
1837–1905

When he was nineteen, Julien Reverchon came from France to join the French Colony at La Réunion near Dallas. While working as a farmer, he gathered 20,000 specimens of plants as a hobby. Most of his collections were sent to the Missouri Botanical Garden in St. Louis, where other botanists saw them and became interested in his work. After exploring much of the Panhandle and West Texas, Reverchon became a professor at Baylor College of Medicine. The genus *Reverchonia* as well as numerous species are named in his honor.

Louis Ervendberg

1809–1863

The botanist Louis Ervendberg is also known as the first German Protestant minister in Texas, arriving in 1839. He established congregations in seven towns. Near New Braunfels he founded an orphanage where he experimented with raising plants new to the area. With seeds from Africa, Arabia, and elsewhere, he grew tobacco, fruits, wheat, corn, grasses, and medicinal plants. Collecting specimens for Harvard University, he found many little known species of plants. As a scientific farmer, he did much to affect the economic growth of Texas.

Author's Notes

p. 1   Although drawings or photographs of most of the early Texas naturalists have been located by the author, none have been found of Louis Berlandier.

p. 3   When Louis Berlandier left Europe for Mexico, he was so excited he forgot to take along his magnifying glass—a most important tool.

p. 3   For every hundred plants in a collection, an early naturalist was paid eight cents per plant.

p. 32   Dr. Asa Gray, a teacher and an authority on plant life, studied and labeled the dried plants that were sent to his Harvard University laboratories. Many plants, previously unknown to scientists, were given their names by Asa Gray.

p. 37   In early Texas when newsprint was scarce, printing was done on more available products such as wallpaper, butcher paper, or pieces of cloth.

p. 63   The island of Galveston was once so infested with snakes that it was called Snake Island.

p. 69   Latin was an important language used and spoken by scholars of the 1800's.

p. 75   John O. Meusebach was the founder of Fredericksburg and the first Texas settler to make a successful treaty with the Comanche Indians. He was also a knowledgeable botanist who experimented with plants to find which ones would grow well in Central Texas.

p. 82   Dr. Lincecum gathered plants for use as medicine.

p. 89   Harvester ants, named by Gideon Lincecum, were also known as Agricultural Ants.

p. 93   At his request, Gideon Lincecum's violin was buried with him. It is within his gravesite at the State Cemetery in Austin.

Glossary

amphibian—any animal that lives both on land and in water.

botanical garden—a place where collections of living and preserved plants and trees are kept and exhibited.

botany—the science that deals with plants, their life, structure, growth, and classification.

classification—the sorting of animals and plants into an order that shows how they are related to each other.

Cretaceous—the time from 140 to 65 million years ago.

fossil—the remains of something that once lived.

genus—(*plural*, **genera**) a group of very closely related plants or animals. A genus may include one or more species. The genus name is capitalized and is followed by the species name, which is not capitalized. Example: *Homo sapiens*, the scientific name for a human being.

geography—the subject concerned with the study of the human and natural features of the earth's surface.

geology—the science dealing with the structure of the earth's crust and the formation and development of its layers. Geology includes the study of rock types and early forms of life found as fossils in rocks.

herbarium—a collection of dried plants that have been mounted and labeled by those who study and identify plant species. Also called 'herbarium' is the building where plant collections are kept. Large herbariums hold 4 million or more species preserved in heavy paper folders and stored in metal cabinets.

lichen—any of a large group of mosslike plants growing in patches on rocks and tree trunks.

Linnaen system—the system of classifying plants and animals by using a double name, the first being that of the genus, and the second the species. Carolus Linnaeus (1707–1778), a Swedish botanist, devised the system, which uses Latin words and/or Latinized names for genus and species names.

mammal—an animal that feeds its young with milk.

medicinal—having the properties of medicine, such as curing, healing, or relieving.

mollusk—an animal with a soft body, usually enclosed in a shell, and having gills and a foot, such as an oyster, clam, mussel, snail, slug, or squid.

natural history—the study of animal and plant life.

naturalist—a person who studies nature, especially by direct observation of animals and plants.

ornithology—the study of birds.

quadruped—an animal, especially a mammal, with four feet.

reptile—a cold-blooded, scaly animal that lays eggs on land, such as a lizard, snake, turtle, or crocodile.

species—a group of plants or animals that share certain characteristics and can reproduce with each other.

specimen—a part of a whole, or one of a class or group, used as a sample or example of the whole, class, or group.

vegetation—plant life in general.

zoology—the science that deals with the classification of animals and the study of animal life.

Suggested Reading

Geiser, Samuel W. *Naturalists of the Frontier.* Dallas: Southern Methodist University Press, 1937.

Burkhalter, Lois. *Gideon Lincecum, A Biography.* Austin: University of Texas Press, 1965.

The Handbook of Texas. Austin: Texas State Historical Association, 1976.

Pool, William C. *A Historical Atlas of Texas.* Austin: Encino Press, 1975.

Roemer, Ferdinand. *Texas.* Waco: Texian Press, 1967.

Wills, Mary M. *Roadside Flowers of Texas.* Austin: University of Texas Press, 1961.

Vines, Robert A. *Trees, Shrubs, and Woody Vines of the Southwest.* Austin: University of Texas Press, 1960.

King, Irene. *John O. Meusebach.* Austin: University of Texas Press, 1967.

Campbell and Loughmiller. *Texas Wildflowers.* Austin: University of Texas Press, 1984.

Ajilvsgi, Geyata. *Wildflowers of Texas.* Bryan: Shearer Publishers, 1984.

Where To See Collections Made By Early Texas Naturalists

Missouri Botanical Gardens	St. Louis, Missouri
New York Historical Society	New York, New York
Stark Museum	Orange, Texas
British Museum	London, England
Museum of Natural History	Budapest, Hungary
Gray Herbarium	Cambridge, Massachusetts
Herbier DeCandolle	Geneva, Switzerland
Royal Botanical Gardens	Kew, England
Botanical Institute	Kiel, Republic of Germany
Natural History Museum	Wien (Vienna), Austria
Smithsonian Institution	Washington, D.C.
Botanic Gardens	Belfast, Ireland
University of Texas	Austin, Texas
Baylor University	Waco, Texas

The museums listed above are only a few of the many places that display such collections. Museums around the world have exhibits in natural history for all ages and levels of interest.

About the Author–Artist

Betsy Warren has an art education degree from Miami University in Ohio and attended the Chicago Art Institute. She has written and illustrated many books for children. Most of them are about her favorite subject, Texas. Her works of historical non-fiction include *Twenty Texans, Indians Who Lived In Texas,* and a *Let's Remember* series of five books about the people and events in Texas history. She also writes for magazines and works as a musician.

Mrs. Warren and her husband have four children and live in Austin, Texas.

About the Researcher

Aline Nemir Speer, born in Austin, Texas, developed an appreciation of nature in childhood during family camping trips along the Comal, Guadalupe, and San Marcos rivers in Central Texas.

Majoring in botany, bacteriology, and zoology, she has a B.A. degree from the University of Texas. From her studies, she was familiar with names of early naturalists but not the details of their lives. Discoveries made during recent research led to collaboration with her neighbor Betsy Warren on *Wilderness Walkers* and *Wildflowers of Texas.*

Mrs. Speer and her husband have one son and live in Austin, Texas.